NOT what it seems

NOT what it seems

Paula Vásquez

GIBBS SMITH
TO ENRICH AND INSPIRE HUMANKIND

this is NOT a
rooster

it is an

alarm
clock

cock-a-doodle-doo

this is NOT an

elephant

it is a

shower

this is NOT a

kangaroo

it is a

shopping cart

this is NOT a

deer

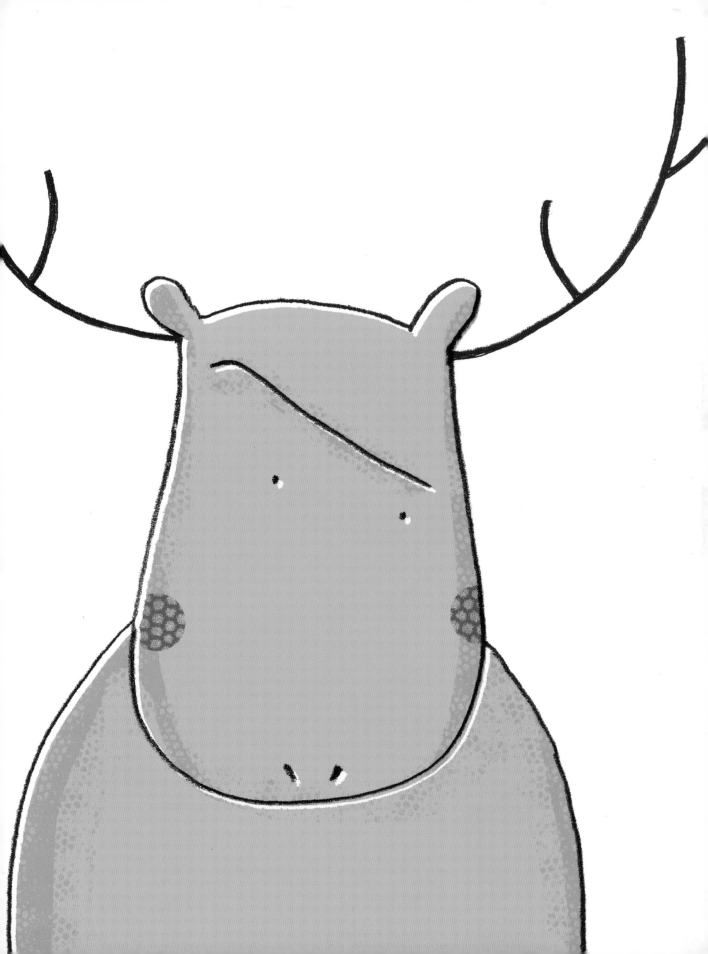

it is a

clothes
hanger

this is NOT a

peacock

it is a

fan

this is NOT a
turtle

it is a

drum

this is NOT an
anteater

it is a
vacuum
cleaner

this is NOT a

canary

it is a
radio

this is NOT a

BOOK

Paula Vásquez, an avowed artist from childhood, studied graphic design at the Universidad Católica de Chile, and honed her illustration skills with a post-graduate diploma from Finis Terrae University. She continued her studies at EINA Escola de Disseny i Art in Barcelona, Spain. She currently lives in Santiago de Chile writing and illustrating children's picture books.

Manufactured in Hong Kong in January 2017 by Paramount Printing, Co.

First Edition
21 20 19 18 17   5 4 3 2 1

Published by
Gibbs Smith
P.O. Box 667
Layton, Utah 84041

1.800.835.4993 orders
www.gibbs-smith.com

Designed by Paula Vásquez
Gibbs Smith books are printed on paper produced from sustainable PEFC-certified forest/controlled wood source. Learn more at www.pefc.org.

Library of Congress Control Number: 2016945728
ISBN: 978-1-4236-4691-4